BARNYARD PRAYERS

LAURA GODWIN
ILLUSTRATED BY BRIAN SELZNICK

HYPERION BOOKS FOR CHILDREN
NEW YORK

For Ann —L.G.
For David —B.S.

Text copyright © 2000 by Laura Godwin

Illustrations copyright © 2000 by Brian Selznick

First Edition

1 3 5 7 9 10 8 6 4 2

Printed in Hong Kong by South China Printing Company, Ltd.

The paintings were prepared in acrylic on unprimed watercolor paper.

Library of Congress Cataloging-in-Publication Data

Barnyard prayers/Godwin, Laura; illustrated by Brian Selznick. — 1st ed.

p. cm.

Summary: A boy's toy farm animals come to life and talk to God in a series of prayers.

ISBN 0-7868-0355-X (trade)

1. Domestic animals—Juvenile poetry. 2. Children's poetry, American. [1. Domestic animals—
Poetry. 2. American poetry. 3. Prayers.] I. Title. II. Selznick, Brian, ill.

PS3557.03155 B37 2000

811'.54 21—DC21

99-040918

Visit www.hyperionchildrensbooks.com, a part of the GO Network

The Farmer's Prayer

Now I lay me down to sleep,
I pray the Lord
My farm to keep.
Bless the sheep, the pigs, the cats,
The spiders, too, the bees and gnats,
The goslings, sparrows, and the hens,
And even the foxes in their dens.
May my cows in splendor graze
And all live peaceful, perfect days.
Watch over us, protected, whole,
And bless this farmer's happy soul.

The Pig's Prayer

Thanks for the farmer
Who keeps me fed,
Scratches my back
And scratches my head.
Thanks for the mud.
Thanks for the rain.
Thanks for the farmer
Once again.

The Spider's Prayer

No rain.
Many flies.
Gentle feet
That take no notice
Of one so small.
That's all.

The Fox's Prayer

Lord in your den above,
I give you thanks
For all the barnyard animals,
Little and sweet—especially
The hens.
I'd sure be grateful
If I could taste
One of them tonight.
One fine fat hen
Is all I ask.
That's not so much.
Why, those hens probably
Wouldn't mind a bit.
Besides, they're so foolish
They'd never notice
If one of their own
Were missing. . . .

The Hens' Prayer

We ask you once again
To watch over us all,
Six, seven, eight,
Nine . . . nine? Amen!

The Cow's Prayer

Lord, I hope my stomachs
Aren't bigger than my eyes,
But how I love each blade of green
That grows beneath thy skies.

The Drones' Prayer

Forgive us, Lord,
For doing nothing all day.
It's just that the worker bees
Are so busy,
We'd only be in the way.
But we thank you for the nectar,
The busy, buzzing hum of the hive,
And the mounds and pounds of pollen
That keep us all alive.
We're glad you made us
A part
Of your sweet honey of a plan.
And God . . .
Save our queen.

The Sparrow's Prayer

Bless us and keep us
And give us this day
Our daily crumbs.

The Colt's Prayer

May my whinny be strong,
My legs, swift,
And my life,
Long.

The Gnat's Prayer

I am a gnat.
I gnaw and I bite
And I LIKE
Things like that.
I fly and I hum
In the horse's ear.
I buzzzz like a bee.
I zzzing and I sting
The pig, the cow,
And the billy goat, too.
That's what I do—
Is it all right
With you?

The Goat's Prayer

I cannot stop
My noisy bleating.
Nor can I help myself
From eating laundry, garbage,
Cans, and such.
And yet, I do not ask for much, save
That my stomach, stalwart still,
Remain as iron as my will.

The Goslings' Prayer

Bless the wild geese that fly,
Our northern cousins.
Grant us eggs that hatch,
And brothers and sisters—
Dozens!

The Duck's Prayer

Thanks for a body
Built to float,
My own little boat
In my own little sea.
Thank you, God,
For making me.

The Dog's Prayer

Help me remember
To beg politely,
To scratch, slightly
(But just for fleas),
To dig outside only
Under the trees,
To bury my bones,
To hamper my howls,
To curb my barks,
To clean my jowls,
To run in circles
And wag my tail,
To sniff and snuffle,
Not slobber and wail.
Lord, help me remember
Things like that
And not to forget
Not to chase the cat.

The Cat's Prayer

Thank you for making me
So beautiful.
My fine whiskers
And shiny coat are like no other's.
The envy of the whole barnyard
Is upon me
And yet, having a generous heart,
I forgive.
How can I blame them for wanting
To be like me?
Why, with my night vision,
Lightning reflexes,
And keen sense of smell,
Even the town animals are talking.
Thanks to you, Lord,
I've got it all.
Oh! Amen, gotta go . . .
Mouse.

The Mouse's Prayer

Think me not a rat and
Please protect me
From the cat.

The Donkey's Prayer

I keep my shaggy watch,
I tend your sheep,
I kick my heels,
I snort,
I paw, Hee-
Haw and say,
"Father in heaven,
Give us this day."
That is how we donkeys pray.

The Sheep's Prayer

I am just a woolly sheep.
Please help me count myself to sleep.

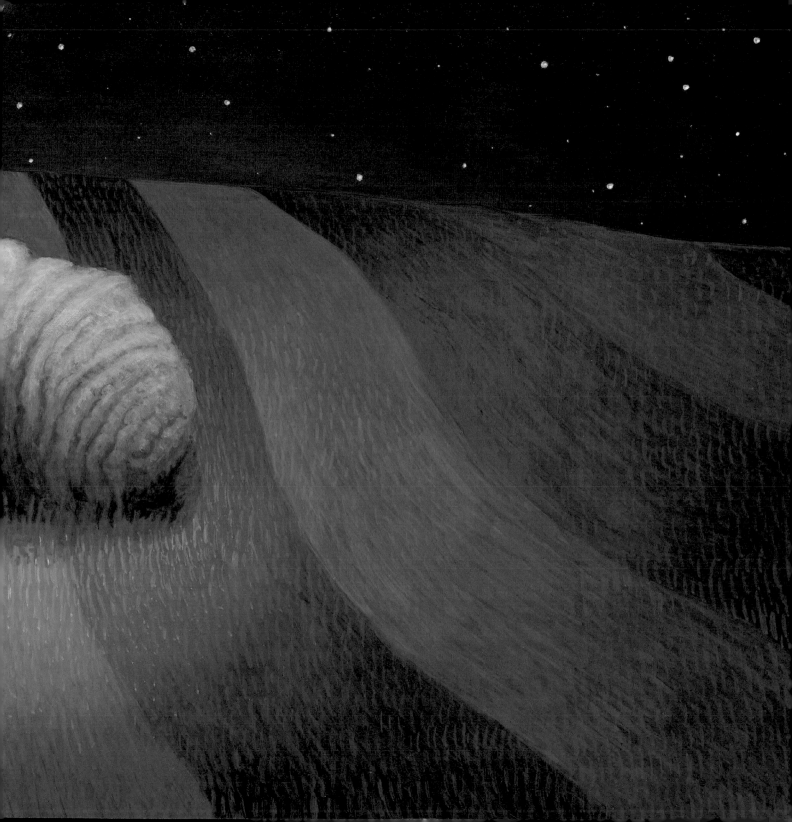

The Farmer's Benediction

Bless these beasts,
Keep them warm,
Free from harm,
Cradled in
Your loving arm.

Amen.